Felicity Wishes®

Pink Paradise

a

Hodder
Children's
Books

A division of Hodder Headline Limited

How to make your felicity Wishes.

W I S H

With this book comes an extra special wish for you and your best friend.

Hold the book together at each end and both close your eyes.

Wriggle your noses and think of a number under ten.

Open your eyes, whisper the numbers you thought of to each other.

Add these numbers together. This is your

Magic Number

you

best friend

Place your little finger on the stars, and say your magic number out loud together. Now make your wish quietly to yourselves. And maybe, one day, your wish might just come true. Love

felicity

x

For Becci Phillips
with lots of sparkly wishes from Auntie Emma x

Emma Thomson's
felicity Wishes®

FELICITY WISHES
Felicity Wishes © 2000 Emma Thomson
Licensed by White Lion Publishing

Text and Illustrations © 2006 Emma Thomson

First published in Great Britain in 2006 by Hodder Children's Books

The right of Emma Thomson to be identified as the author and illustrator of this work has
been asserted by her in accordance with the Copyright, Designs and Patents Act 1988.

l

A Catalogue record for this book is available from the British Library

ISBN 0 340 91193 X

Printed and bound in Great Britain by Bookmarque Ltd, Croydon, Surrey

The paper and board used in this paperback by Hodder Children's Books are natural recyclable
products made from wood grown in sustainable forests. The manufacturing processes
conform to the environmental regulations of the country of origin.

Hodder Children's Books
A division of Hodder Headline Ltd, 338 Euston Road, London NW1 3BH

CONTENTS

Feathered Friend

Felicity Wishes was feeling strange. It had been raining in Little Blossoming for five days in a row and everything, including Felicity's mood, was a little grey.

"It's unlike you not to be full of sparkle," said Polly, as they stood sheltered from the rain under the Large Oak Tree.

"I know," said Felicity, shuffling her feet in a muddy puddle. "I just feel out of sorts, and I can't put my wand on why."

"It's the weather," said Polly resolutely. "It makes even the happiest fairies' wings droop."

"Who's got droopy wings?" burst out Holly, landing with a splash beside them.

"Not you!" laughed Daisy, admiring Holly's latest fashion accessory. Holly was incredibly fashion-conscious. Being up to date with fairy trends meant that she was sporting a pair of Marvellous Miraculous Waterproof Wings.

"Where in Fairy World did you get those?" asked Felicity, wide-eyed.

"Wings and Things," beamed Holly, spinning round to give her friends a better look and splashing mud all over Felicity's legs and skirt.

Felicity sighed and shrugged her shoulders. She was feeling too droopy even to get upset.

"The weather forecast for tomorrow is sunshine for a week, so I've got to get my wear out of these while I can!" And, with that, Holly was off.

* * *

The next day, sunshine burst through Felicity's bedroom curtains with a light so golden it could make anyone's heart sing. But not Felicity's. By the time she got to school her wings had drooped so deeply that they were almost dragging on the floor. Even her hair fell limp on her shoulders.

"New hairdo?" asked Daisy innocently.

"No," said Felicity. "It's lost its

bounce and so have I. I don't know what's the matter. It's not like anything's happened to make me feel blue."

Suddenly she spun round in a panic, finally realizing what was wrong. "It's my bird!" she cried. "Bertie's gone! I knew there had to be a reason for me feeling so out of sorts!"

Bertie Dishes was Felicity's blue bird. He'd been flying along beside her ever since she could remember. In his own quiet way, Bertie looked out for Felicity, gently steering her away from danger with his soft feathers. And even though, most of the time, Felicity barely noticed he was there, she felt lost without him.

"How terrible!" said Felicity in

disbelief. "I've been feeling strange without him for days and I've only just noticed that he's gone!"

"Where do you think he is?" ventured Daisy.

"I don't know! He's never left me before, not even for a minute."

"Can you remember the last time you saw him?"

"No! Well, I know he was with me at school last Thursday, because he helped me when I got lost on the way to our science lesson," said Felicity.

"Wasn't that the day when you had a bit of a disaster in class?" asked Holly, trying to control her giggles. Miss Sparkle hadn't been very impressed when Felicity had caused an explosion in chemistry class that day.

"I wouldn't really call it a disaster, more of a mishap," said Felicity, blushing.

"Anyway, let's retrace your steps and

see whether we can find Bertie!" said Daisy, tactfully changing the subject.

"Good idea!" replied Felicity, feeling better already.

They searched absolutely everywhere – under tables, in cupboards, between the coats in the cloakroom – but still there was no sign of Bertie. He seemed to have vanished!

Felicity found the afternoon's lessons more difficult than normal. And she couldn't help feeling it was because Bertie wasn't there.

"Lift your wings up and do try to concentrate!" said Miss Meandering, the geography teacher, as she bent down to lift Felicity out of the ditch.

"It's very important to look at where you're going as well as at the compass!"

"Yes, miss," Felicity sighed. "I bet if Bertie had been here I wouldn't have made such a fool of myself," she murmured.

She felt she'd be safe in her next class, cookery, but without Bertie by her side it was worse than she could have imagined.

"Oh, really, Felicity!" said Miss Olive, exasperated. "It's one thing to knead the dough, but kneeling in the dough is quite another thing entirely."

"Sorry, miss," said Felicity sheepishly. "I sort of slipped."

* * *

"What happened to you?" giggled Holly as Felicity approached the school gate.

Felicity looked down at the hole in her tights and brushed the flour from her nose as Daisy carefully pulled a leaf from her crown.

"Being Bertie-less. That's what's happened to me!" said Felicity, managing half a smile. "I never realized how much I relied on him being there. And now he's gone." Her eyes welled up with tears. "I don't know what to do."

"I'll tell you what we'll do!" said Polly, who was always very sensible. "We'll keep looking for him. And when we find him, you'll soon be back to your usual self. We're your friends, and none of us likes to see you sad."

* * *

So Holly, Polly, Daisy and Felicity picked up their search where they left off that morning.

Holly was the one to spot Felicity's feathered friend first, in the park.

"Look!" she squealed. "Bertie! Look! I can see him!"

"Where?" cried Felicity, squinting into the distance.

"There!" said Polly. "I saw him too. Just for a second! He was over by that bush, I saw his  bright-blue feathers!"

But Felicity was gone, flying at speed towards an area where dozens of fairies were playing, reading and relaxing in the afternoon sun. The closer she got, the faster her heart beat. She could see Bertie dipping in and out of the sky every few seconds, disappearing behind the bush. "I wonder what he's doing," she thought to herself as she flapped furiously. "And he's certainly put on weight in the time he's been away from me – his tummy looks positively round!"

The closer Felicity got to the bush, the rounder and bigger Bertie's tummy became… until she could see that it wasn't Bertie at all, but a small blue beach ball being tossed into the air by her friend Winnie!

"Want to play?" asked Winnie, spotting Felicity staring open-mouthed at her ball.

"Um, no thanks!" said Felicity, deeply disappointed. "I thought your ball was my blue bird! I don't suppose you've seen him?"

"You could try the pond down by the green," said Winnie helpfully. "There are always lots of birds down there."

"Thanks!" said Felicity, heading back to her friends. "Perhaps that was it, perhaps Bertie had had enough of hanging around with fairies and wanted to spend some time with his own bird friends," she thought.

"It makes sense," said Daisy, when Felicity shared her idea. "Let's go there now and find out."

Felicity and her friends could hear the birds by the pond even before they saw them. Pretty whistling tunes carried through the air for miles. Their songs always filled Little Blossoming with music that Felicity had, up until then, taken for granted.

"I think I can hear Bertie's voice!" cried Felicity. "He loves nursery rhymes – listen!"

Holly, Polly and Daisy stopped flapping their wings for a second while they listened. They could hear the notes of "Baa, Baa, Black Sheep".

"Yes!" said Holly. "I recognize that tune! It's Bertie, it must be. No other birds I know sing like that."

And again Felicity was off, speeding ahead of the others to greet her lost friend.

When Polly, Daisy and Holly caught up with her, Felicity was looking down in the dumps again.

"Wasn't it him?" asked Polly, looking over her friend's shoulder.

Felicity nodded glumly towards the nearby ice cream van.

"Is he getting an ice cream?" ventured Daisy.

"No, silly!" said Felicity. "It wasn't Bertie singing nursery rhymes, it was the ice cream van's music!"

"Oh, Felicity!" said Polly giving her friend a great big hug. "I'm afraid our search isn't proving to be very successful."

"Let's have an ice cream to cheer ourselves up," suggested Holly.

FAIRY WHIPPY

ICE CREAM

Quietly they all sat by the pond eating their ice creams. Dazed, Felicity studied her cone. Suddenly, she had an idea. "Being here by the water eating an ice cream has made me think about the beach."

"What," said Holly, "you think Bertie's gone on holiday?"

"Maybe," said Felicity. "He's never migrated before, but there's a first time for everything."

"But how will you find him?" asked Polly. "He could be on the other side of Fairy World by now."

"I don't know. I'll keep looking, but until I find him I'm just going to have to try very hard to look after myself," said Felicity, popping the last bit of the cone into her mouth and missing.

✳ ✳ ✳

Over the next few days Felicity took extra care in everything she did. She tried earnestly not to become distracted with thoughts of her lost friend and concentrate on the task at hand, but to little effect.

Each day brought a new catastrophe and by Thursday morning Felicity was a walking disaster. Her wand was broken from tumbling down the stairs,  her crown was bent from tripping over her bag, and her favourite pair of stripy tights was covered in holes.

"Felicity, I've never seen you looking so messy before!" said Daisy, staring at her untidy friend.

"I know. I keep looking out for Bertie, instead of watching where I'm going or concentrating on what I'm doing!" she confessed to Daisy as they sat down in science class.

"Don't worry, Felicity," said Daisy.

"I'm sure he'll come back to you soon."

"It was this time last week that I last remember seeing Bertie," Felicity sighed, pointing to two tiny footprints on the book in front of her. "I remember it well because I caused the most enormous explosion with my invisibility powder. Miss Sparkle made me stay behind after school and clean the mess up!"

"So you had mishaps even when Bertie was around," mused Holly.

"Just not quite so many!" giggled Daisy.

"I suppose so," said Felicity, pulling herself together and sitting up straight. "But I'm not going to have any more, Bertie or no Bertie."

And she listened to Miss Sparkle so intently that the teacher wondered if something was wrong!

It was when the class had reached a critical point in their experiments that Felicity's concentration suddenly wavered. Outside the window, perched on top of the school fence, was definitely something blue. Felicity couldn't be sure, but she thought, as she got up on tiptoe, that it just might be Bertie.

"Now be very careful, class – this fairy magic powder is very powerful. We don't want any accidents again!" called Miss Sparkle, looking pointedly at Felicity.

At that very moment, Felicity lost her balance. She reached out to steady herself, but it was too late! With one arm holding the delicate magic powder, Felicity crashed heavily against Polly.

In what seemed like slow motion, Polly lost hold of her powder and it flew high into the air and smashed into Felicity's magic powder. Miss Sparkle watched aghast. She barely had time to shout "DUCK!" before the chemistry lab was filled with an enormous bang! Crowns flew off, wands shot through the air and wings were singed with the whirling, sparkling powder.

✳ ✳ ✳

When everyone who had been able to hide crawled out from under their desks, and those that had not hidden unstuck themselves from the ceiling, tears were rolling down Felicity's face.

"Now, now!" said Miss Sparkle, straightening her crown. "There's no need for tears. The mess you made with the invisibility powder last week was much worse than the accident you've had here today, Felicity."

Felicity continued to sob.

"Really, Felicity. Don't be sad.

Everything can be fixed," she said. She looked at her wand, and then less certainly at the wands of the other fairies in the class.

"I-I-I-I-I'm not crying because I'm sad," spluttered Felicity. "These are tears of joy!"

Miss Sparkle frowned.

"I've found Bertie!" said Felicity, and she beamed an enormous sparkling smile.

Miss Sparkle stepped carefully over the mess on the floor and made her way over to Felicity's desk, where a small blue bird was whistling nursery rhymes.

"But where's he come from?"

exclaimed Daisy.
"We've been
looking for
him for days!"

"I think
I know!"
mused Polly.
"I don't think
him appearing during the science
lesson was a coincidence."

"What do you mean?" asked Holly.

"Well, I'm just wondering whether
the invisibility powder took effect on
Bertie during last week's mishap. And
now he's been made visible again by
whatever magic Felicity accidentally
just performed!"

"I'm sure you're right!" said Miss
Sparkle. "A perfect example of the
lesson I was teaching you. Felicity
was clearly wishing very strongly for
Bertie to come back. It just goes to
prove what I'm always telling you.

Magic powder is important, but not as powerful as the wish it helps to come true!"

"And Bertie never left me," said Felicity, hugging her blue bird. "Even when you think friends are far away, they never really are."

friends are
never far away

because they're
always in your heart

Pink Paradise

Felicity Wishes' friend Winnie was
shaking as she stumbled into
registration class that morning.

"Your wings are all-of-a-quiver!"
said Felicity, fluttering over to greet
her. "Do you want to borrow my
cardigan?"

"I'm not cold," said Winnie, whose
voice was a little shaky too. "I've just
had some really exciting news! Look!"
she said, pulling out a large sparkly
envelope from her bag.

As Felicity read the contents of the

letter her wings started to jiggle too!

"Oh, Winnie!" she gasped. "This is wonderful news! I'm so pleased for you. You'll be able to put all your adventuring talents to the test!"

Winnie, who wanted to be an Adventure Fairy when she graduated from the School of Nine Wishes, had been offered a weekend job at a brand-new adventure park that was opening just outside Little Blossoming.

"I know!" said Winnie. "Just think of all the things I can suggest. I've been up all night scribbling down ideas." She excitedly showed Felicity her notebook.

"There's just one thing I can't decide on. It needs something to bring all the rides and features together. You know, like a desert-island theme, or a spaceship theme," said Winnie, chewing the end of her pen.

Felicity closed her eyes and thought.

Suddenly, Bertie, Felicity's blue bird, who had heard the entire conversation from Felicity's shoulder, tugged playfully at her pink cardigan.

"No, Bertie!" said Felicity giggling. "Winnie's already said that she's not cold, just excited!"

Bertie shook his head and continued to tug.

"What are you trying to say?" asked Felicity, who was struggling to interpret Bertie's tweets. "A cardigan theme park? It's a lovely idea, but somehow I can't see it working."

Frustrated, Bertie shook his head again and dived into Felicity's bag.

He pulled out her favourite pink pen.

"A drawing theme for the park?" she questioned. "I don't think so, Bertie. We need a theme that all fairies will love."

Bertie was exasperated. Flapping his wings, he gently tugged at the pink ribbon in Winnie's hair.

"Oh, look! He thinks your hair ribbon is a worm!" giggled Felicity. "But I'll tell you something … it's given me a fantastic idea. What about having a 'Pink' theme?"

Winnie clapped her hands with glee, and Bertie raised his eyes to the sky – it's what he'd been trying to say all along.

"That's a wonderful thought!" Winnie said, barely able to contain her excitement. "And it will work so well with all my ideas."

* * *

Welcome to the Land of Pink theme park!
A glittery pink path leads you round twelve features,
stalls and rides, all designed to give you the ultimate pink experience.
Visit a minimum of three of these to ensure a totally pink day. Enjoy!

1. Pink Outfits – Not wearing pink today? Visit this stall to choose an entirely pink outfit.

2. Pink Hair – Fancy a change that will tickle you pink? Choose from over a hundred different shades of pink to find the one to suit you!

3. Pink Ice Cream – Having a pink day is hungry work! Visit stall three for strawberry, bubblegum and marshmallow flavoured ice cream.

4. Pink Ride – Climb to the top of the pink candyfloss mountain in an open-top pink carriage and feast your eyes on breathtaking views.

5. Pink Personality – You're all pink on the outside, now be pink on the inside with a workshop to make you bubblegum bubbly!

6. Paint Pink – Why paint the town red, when it would be so much nicer pink? Create your very own pink masterpiece to frame on your wall and help you remember today for ever.

7. Pink Swim – Splash and have fun in our pink swimming pool, in your very own complimentary pink swimming costume.

8. Pink Dreams – Feeling a bit tired after all your pink adventures? Relax and unwind in our Pink Dreams chill-out zone.

9. Pink Rollercoaster – Come and have fun on a ride that will make the butterflies in your tummy turn pink.

10. Pink Chute – Ride on an enormous pink lollipop at speeds that will make your heart leap and turn your cheeks pink!

11. Pink Makeover – Delicate pinks for your eyes, rose-pinks for your lips and a soft dusting of pink blusher to make your look complete.

12. Pink Sunset – Choose to enjoy this adventure just as the sun goes down and rest on a cloud bathed in magical pink light.

Over the next few months Felicity and her friends, Holly, Polly and Daisy, didn't see much of Winnie. Each break-time she was in the library working out more adventures to include in the Land of Pink theme park. And every evening after school she went to the building site where hundreds of fairies were making her ideas real.

It was only in double maths that Felicity finally caught up on Winnie's latest news.

"Close your eyes," said Winnie excitedly as Felicity sat down beside her, "and put your hands out."

Felicity did as she was told. Surprises were one of her favourite things.

Holly, Polly and Daisy peeped over Felicity's shoulder, eager to see the surprise.

"OK!" said Winnie, barely able to

contain her excitement.
"You can open them
now!"

Felicity quickly
opened her eyes to
see four glittering
pink tickets.

"I'd like you, Holly,
Polly and Daisy to be
the first to visit the
theme park. The grand open day is
next Saturday. I hope you can all
come!"

* * *

Felicity and her friends couldn't think
of anything else for the rest of the
week and when Saturday finally came
they were ready to explode with
excitement.

Winnie was standing proudly by the
gate, ready to greet them.

"The first thing I have to give you is
this," she said, handing leaflets to

Holly, Polly, Daisy and Felicity. "On one side are the instructions on how

to use the park, and on the other
side is a map in case you get lost."

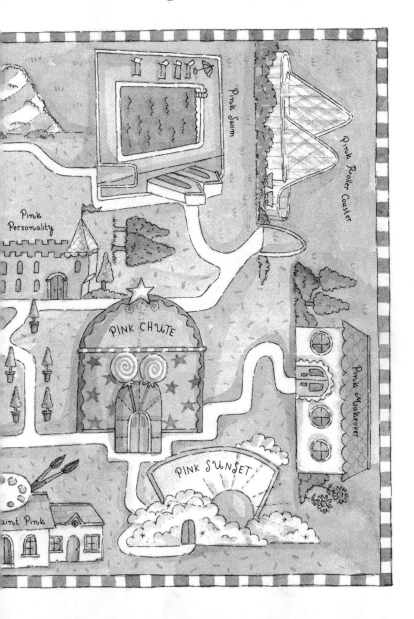

Felicity, Holly, Polly and Daisy stood wide-eyed, looking at their maps.

"I don't know what to choose first!" said Felicity to her friends. "I want to do them all!"

Bertie tapped his beak along the writing at the top.

"Oh, it says here to do a minimum of three things," continued Felicity, reading her sheet carefully. "I guess you'd never have time to do them all in one day."

"That's right," said Winnie. "We designed the Land of Pink so that you could come time and time again and each visit you could have a different combination and leave with a completely new pink experience!"

"How fantastic!" said Holly, who had already decided on her three treats of the day.

"What are we waiting for? Let's

start!" cried Polly, as she led the way under the large pink arch that formed the entrance to the park.

* * *

"I can't believe my eyes!" said Felicity, spinning round and round on the spot and covering Bertie with her hair. "Everything is pink! The flowers, the path, the staff uniforms, even the sky!"

"I've got to get a pink outfit quick!" said Holly, feeling out of place in her red dress.

"Me too!" said Daisy, looking down at the pretty blue flowers that decorated her skirt.

"Well, I don't think I need a pink outfit," giggled Felicity. Her favourite colour was pink and she was rarely seen dressed in anything else! "I'm off to get a pink hairdo!"

"Why don't we all meet by Pink Ice Cream in an hour?" suggested Polly,

who still hadn't decided what she
wanted to do first.

* * *

It was a while before the four fairy
friends recognized each other at the
ice cream bar.

Felicity had opted not for a wig in
the end, but a semi-permanent pink
bubble perm.

Holly and Daisy looked positively
rosy in their new pink dresses and
Polly returned with a pink makeover
that everyone was envious of.

"I'm going there next!" said Felicity, looking carefully at the delicate pink eyeshadow that dusted Polly's eyelids. "You look beautiful!"

"Well, I'm going on the Pink Chute next!" announced Holly, pointing to the ride behind them. "Who wants to join me?"

"Me!" said Daisy, jumping up and down as she watched the carriage hurtle down the ride. "It looks like fun!"

"Me too!" said Polly.

"Well, by the looks of the queue you'll still be there by the time I've finished my makeover, so I'll come and find you when you're done," suggested Felicity.

* * *

Felicity's makeover was dreamy. As she sat in a tall, ornate, golden and pink velvet chair, two fairies brought her tray after tray of eyeshadows,

43

lipsticks and blushers in every shade of pink you could imagine. For her eyes, she chose to have a rainbow that went from the lightest, most delicate pink through to a deep cherry pink. For her cheeks, she chose two tones of pink blusher that perfectly complemented the rosebud lipgloss.

After her makeover was complete, Felicity skipped towards the Pink Chute. Out of the corner of her eye, she noticed something very exciting.

Felicity looked at her watch. The queue to the Pink Chute was long and her makeover had been very quick. She was sure she had enough time for a quick go on the Pink Ride before she met her friends...

* * *

Holly, Polly and Daisy stood shaking off the sparkledust after their ride had finished.

"That was fantastic!" giggled Holly, showering her friends with glitter as she flicked her hair.

"It was great fun, but I'm pooped! How about going to Pink Dreams to relax when Felicity gets here?" suggested Polly.

"Good idea!" said Daisy, looking at her map. "You know, the Pink Dreams chill-out zone is right next door to the makeover parlour. If we walk over there now, we are bound to bump into Felicity."

But by the time the fairies got over to the chill-out zone, no one had caught sight of their fairy friend. And when Daisy popped next door to the makeover parlour, the beauty fairies said that Felicity had left ten minutes ago.

Meanwhile, Felicity had been climbing the pink candyfloss mountain in an open-topped pink carriage. She stared at the views with such a wide-open mouth that at one point Bertie, her blue bird, nearly flew inside!

Suddenly the carriage came to a stop.

"How lovely that the ride stops for a break here," Felicity said casually to Bertie. "It must be so you can enjoy the view. I can see everything from here! There's the makeover parlour, the pink-dress stall, the pink swimming pool and the chill-out zone."

"Oh, goodness! There are Holly, Polly and Daisy," cried Felicity, as she frantically tried to catch her friends' attention. "Their ride must have finished already."

She looked around her carriage for a button to continue the ride and take her back down the candyfloss mountain to meet her friends.

"Surely it can't be broken," she said, reluctant to think the worst.

But Bertie had already discovered the terrible truth.

As loudly as he could, he whistled to get Felicity's attention. The carriage wheels were stuck fast in pink candyfloss goo!

"Oh, dear!" said Felicity, inspecting the damage and popping a little candyfloss into her mouth just to make sure it was real. "I shall have to push us out of this mess."

Using all the wing power she could muster, Felicity pushed, and pushed, and pushed the carriage, but it would not budge. Exhausted by all her efforts, she lay back in the soft candyfloss to catch her breath.

"It's no good!" she said to Bertie. "The carriage is stuck! I shall have to fly back to get help."

But when Felicity tried to get up, she found that the carriage wasn't the only thing that was stuck. Her wings were cemented to the candyfloss like glue!

✳ ✳ ✳

Back on the ground in the Pink Dreams chill-out zone, Holly, Polly and Daisy were getting worried.

"They've called for her over the tannoy, but Felicity's nowhere to be seen," said Holly, plonking herself down in a pink chair. "I've checked all the other stalls, rides and features, and there's no sign of her there either."

"It's hopeless!" said Polly, getting quite upset. "Felicity's usually so easy to spot because of her pink dress, but here she just blends into the background, especially with her new pink hair!"

Large tears welled up in Polly's eyes and one began to fall down her cheek. Out of nowhere, a soft feathery touch brushed it away.

"Bertie!" exclaimed Polly. "Where did you come from? Where's Felicity?"

Bertie tweeted with all his might.

"I don't understand," said Holly, looking at the bird quizzically. "Does anyone else?"

Daisy shrugged.

"He's definitely trying to tell us something," said Polly, as she turned to face the little blue bird who was pecking frantically at the chill-out zone menu.

"Do you think he's hungry?" asked Daisy.

"It looks like he wants us to order him some candyfloss," said Holly.

Suddenly Bertie flew up from the

table and headed out of the door.

"I think he wants us to follow him," said Daisy, grabbing her wand.

Daisy, Polly and Holly followed Bertie through the crowds of pink fairies.

"It is a good job Bertie is blue, otherwise he would be lost in all this pink and we would never be able to follow him," said Holly, walking briskly behind her friends.

Suddenly Bertie stopped.

"Oh, my goodness," said Polly, looking up into the sky. "Candyfloss mountain! Are you telling us that Felicity is stuck on candyfloss mountain?"

Bertie gave his loudest tweet yet.

Holly, Polly, and Daisy stood looking up at the enormous pink mountain that dominated the entire theme park.

"That candyfloss is as pink as

Felicity," said Holly, shading her eyes to get a better look. "We'll never find her!"

Just then Bertie spread his beautiful bright-blue wings and began to fly up to the very top of the mountain. Holly's, Polly's and Daisy's eyes followed Bertie as he flew higher and higher.

CANDYFLOSS
MOUNTAIN

Suddenly, glimmering in the sunlight, right at the top of the mountain, Holly, Polly and Daisy saw a tiny pink speck frantically waving.

"It's Felicity!" gasped Polly.

With Winnie's help it was only a matter of minutes before a rescue party had been dispatched to bring Felicity safely back down.

"I'm SO pleased to be back on the ground!" said Felicity, giving all her friends a big sticky hug. "But I'm even more pleased because I've made a very important decision."

"What?" asked Polly. "That you'll never eat candyfloss again?"

"No!" giggled Felicity. "I've decided... that my second-favourite colour is... BLUE!"

And Bertie blushed a delicate shade of pink.

Bertie Blues

Felicity Wishes and her friends, Holly, Polly and Daisy, were spending a lazy afternoon lying in the sunshine, drinking ice cream milkshakes and listening to the Fairy Top Hundred singles chart on the radio in Daisy's garden. Susie Sparkle's brand-new track had been released that week and they were all dying to know whether it had reached number one.

"WOW! I knew she could do it!"

squealed Felicity, springing to her feet and starting to dance.

"Straight in at number one!" said Holly, joining in the dance routine.

"She really is a fairy superstar!" burst out Polly, doing a little magic hip wiggle that ended in a twist.

"Watch my flo—" shouted Daisy. But before Daisy had time to say the word "flowers", Felicity, Holly and Polly had already discoed their way all over them!

"Oh, no!" cried Daisy, rushing towards her flower bed. "My prize petunias are ruined!"

Felicity, Holly and Polly stopped dancing and looked at where they were standing.

"Oh, goodness!" said Felicity, seeing the mess they had made.

"Whoops!" said Holly, lifting her feet carefully out of the soil.

"These petunias were going to be part of a display for the annual Little Blossoming Flower Show," sobbed Daisy.

"We're really sorry, Daisy," said Felicity, putting an arm around her friend. "Don't worry, we'll help you grow some more. And I'm sure the new ones will look even more beautiful than these did."

Daisy looked up at Felicity and across at Holly and Polly, who were still feeling very guilty and couldn't look Daisy in the eye.

"I'm afraid there's no time," said Daisy, trying to control her sobs. "The show is the week after next. The whole display is centred around the petunias, and now there are none I shall have to pull out of the show."

"What about if we created another display?" suggested Polly sensibly. "You have a wonderful garden, full of flowers just waiting to bloom."

Daisy was reluctant to let go of the dream she had had for the last few months: winning first prize at the show with her petunias.

"I don't know…" she said, her voice tailing off. "The only other flowers I have are all still in bud. It would take an awful lot of tender loving care to get them to open in time to make a new display effective."

"It's the least we can do," said Felicity, knowing Holly and Polly agreed.

✳ ✳ ✳

Letting go of her original dream was a difficult thing for Daisy to do. After her friends had left she sat down quietly on her grass and looked at all the beautiful buds that surrounded her. She tried hard to imagine that the potential they had inside them would be as wonderful as her poor squashed petunias.

Slowly and thoughtfully she got up and walked around the garden with her pen and notebook in her hand.

It wasn't long before a big beaming smile had replaced the sad frown she'd started with.

"I've got it!" she giggled down the phone to Felicity. "Tell the others and I'll meet you in Sparkles in half an hour."

* * *

Daisy excitedly showed her new ideas to her friends. The new floral display would focus on a very rare campanula, surrounded by sweet williams, bluebells and foxgloves. It would be wonderful.

"Perhaps," said Daisy tentatively to

her friends, "even more wonderful than the petunias would have been."

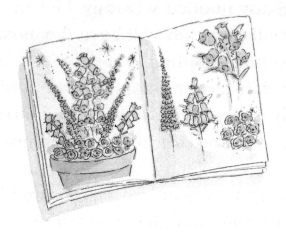

Carefully, Daisy brought out the pots filled with the precious budding plants she'd chosen to give each of her friends. Under her watchful tuition and specific instruction the flowers would, with luck, open in time for the flower show.

"The foxgloves are for you," said Daisy to Holly, "and the sweet williams are for you Polly."

"Surely you're not giving the campanula to me?" said Felicity, whose gardening skills were less than average.

Daisy nodded seriously. "When they flower they will have the most beautiful bluebell-shaped petals. In the wild they wouldn't flower until July, but with your love and a little bit of magic they should open just in time for the show."

Felicity winced. "Maybe I could look after something less important?"

"I'm definitely sure I want you to look after these," said Daisy resolutely. "And for one very special reason."

Felicity looked quizzically at Daisy.

"Your little blue bird, Bertie."

"My blue bird?" asked Felicity, noting that Bertie had fluffed up his feathers and was now sitting on her crown, listening intently to Daisy.

"Nature has a very special way of encouraging flowers to reach their full potential," continued Daisy.

Felicity nodded, though still confused.

"Campanula normally live in woodland, surrounded by birds, just like Bertie. It is thought that their sweet tunes encourage the flowers to grow. So you see, I do need you to look after them."

Felicity suddenly felt superfluous.

"Is there anything left for me to do?" she asked quietly.

"Oh, yes," said Daisy, noting her friend's disappointment. "You have the most important job of all. To keep the flowers watered and bathed in every single drop of love and sunshine you can give them."

Felicity beamed at the precious campanula buds.

* * *

For the next few weeks Felicity, Holly, Polly and Daisy tended their young plants tirelessly until at last tiny flashes of colour began to burst through the buds.

At the end of the week, the fairy friends met in Sparkles to catch up on the progress of their flowers.

"It's going to look amazing," said Holly, slurping her blueberry milkshake.

"It will if the flowers open in the next couple of days," said Daisy, who was secretly very worried.

"My sweet williams look as though they will be open any moment!" announced Polly excitedly. "I can't wait to walk around the flower show and know that I contributed to something everyone will be admiring."

"Eight of my twelve buds are already open!" said Holly proudly.

"That's great, Holly," said Daisy,

feeling a little perkier. "And what about the campanula, Felicity?"

"Nothing," she sighed, "but Bertie has been singing to them every morning and we even slept outside with them last night so that he would be able to sing his song as soon as the sun rose."

"They are the centrepiece of the whole display. They have to be ready in time!"

"I'm sure they will be," said Felicity, trying to reassure herself as much as Daisy.

* * *

When Felicity and Bertie arrived home that afternoon they discovered that the first of the flowers had opened fully.

"Come and look, Bertie," said Felicity excitedly, leaning over to look more closely at the flowers. "They're beautiful! And their perfume is more magical and delicate than I could have dreamed!"

But when Bertie hovered closely so he could smell their delicate perfume, he sneezed the most enormous sneeze!

"Surely you can't have a cold, Bertie," said Felicity. "It's the middle of summer!"

* * *

The next morning, Felicity woke bright and early. She jumped out of bed and flung open her pretty pink curtains.

"Bertie!" Felicity called up to her bird. "Bertie, come quickly!" she urged.

But Bertie wasn't feeling very well.

When Felicity called him a third time and he still didn't respond, she went to find him.

"Oh, Bertie," gasped Felicity at her friend. He was still tucked up in bed, frantically sneezing. "Poor you!" she said fondly, as she sat down on the edge of the bed and gently stroked his feathers.

"I was calling you to say that all the buds have opened! Just in time, too! But you look far too poorly to come down to the garden. I know, I'll bring them up to you!" And with that, Felicity was off.

She returned to the bedroom with the campanula plants as soon as she could.

Bertie sneezed again.

"There," she said, setting the pot down beside him, "these should make you feel better." But Bertie didn't feel better. As the afternoon went on not only was Bertie non-stop sneezing, but his eyes were non-stop watering too!

* * *

Later on that afternoon, Polly and Holly called round to collect the campanulas from Felicity for the next day's show.

"Poor Bertie," said Polly to Felicity, looking down at him in bed.

"He seems to be getting worse," said Felicity. "I'm really sorry, but I don't think I'll be able to come to the flower show tomorrow."

"But you must!" urged Polly. "The flowers you tended are going to be the centre of attention and if we win, so will you!"

Felicity thought hard. She knew that Bertie would be OK if she went, but she also knew that he would never leave her if she was feeling unwell.

"Well, I think you're over indulging him!" said Holly firmly to Felicity when they were safely out of Bertie's earshot. "I suggest that you get him out of bed and take him outside for some fresh air. I'm sure a little sunshine will cheer him up and you'll be able to come after all."

"Do you think so?" asked Felicity, a little uncertain.

"Anything is worth a go, isn't it?" asked Polly, as she picked up the campanulas and headed out of the front door. "It would be terrible if you weren't able to come tomorrow."

Felicity didn't want to miss the show or let her friends down, so she carefully carried Bertie outside into the garden and laid him down in the middle of two large fluffy cushions. She put his favourite birdseed treats by his side and tuned the radio to Bird FM.

But Bertie had been in the chair for less than five minutes before his sneezes and tears became worse than ever.

"Poor Bertie," thought Felicity, trying to put herself in his place. "Perhaps a change of scene will cheer him up."

Felicity heaved out the wheelbarrow, carefully popped her friend on top of the soft fresh grass cuttings that filled it and proceeded to push Bertie around the garden, past the roses, through the daisies and around the honeysuckle. The quicker Felicity pushed, the more she thought Bertie was enjoying himself.

After Felicity and Bertie had circled the garden dozens of times, they collapsed in a heap on the ground. Felicity was in fits of giggles but she soon noticed that Bertie was looking far from better.

* * *

The next morning Felicity made a phone call she had been putting off since the day before.

"Don't worry, Felicity," said Daisy. "It's a real shame after all the hard work you've put in, but I completely understand. I would do the same thing if any of my flowers were sick. I'll take lots of photos for you."

"Thanks," said Felicity, feeling a

little better. "Promise to come round afterwards and tell me all about it?"

"I promise!" said Daisy, hanging up the phone.

Felicity was secretly devastated, though she tried not to let her feelings show in front of Bertie. She was determined to have a fun day no matter how sad she felt that she was missing the show.

"Today," said Felicity to Bertie, "is going to be a great day!"

Felicity spent most of the morning telling Bertie silly bird stories and even sillier bird jokes.

"What do you get if you cross a cat with a parrot?" asked Felicity, giggling already.

Bertie opened one eye and shrugged. "A carrot!"

Bertie giggled and then sneezed.

* * *

Later on that afternoon it took Felicity

so long to get to the door that Holly, Polly and Daisy were just about to give up and walk away.

"What in Fairy World have you got on?" gasped Holly, looking at Felicity's unusual outfit.

Felicity was giggling so hysterically that the cardboard beak she had tied to her nose fell off!

"I've been entertaining Bertie," she said, stepping back to let her friends in. "My bird impressions needed some help to make them more convincing."

And Felicity gave her friends a little twirl so they could see the full effect of her home-made bird outfit!

"And that's not all!" she urged, taking Polly by the hand and leading her friends to the kitchen. "We've been busy baking too!" Holly, Polly and Daisy looked at an enormous plate of cookies.

Holly's tummy rumbled at the sight

of food after a long day at the show. Before Felicity had a chance to protest, Holly popped a biscuit in her mouth.

"Uuuuuuughhhhh!" yelled Holly, spitting biscuit everywhere.

Felicity tried hard not to giggle. "They're get-better biscuits for Bertie!" she smiled, showing the others. "I made them today... out of birdseed!"

Holly put her hand over her mouth. "I didn't think your cooking was normally this bad!" she said, still pulling a rather peculiar face as the flavour of the birdseed biscuit lingered in her mouth.

"Don't you want to know how it went?" asked Daisy.

"How what went?" asked Felicity blankly, as she sat down next to Bertie.

"The flower show, silly!" said Polly.

"Oh, my goodness, yes!" gasped Felicity. "Bertie and I have had so much fun here, I'd forgotten all about it. How did the campanulas look? Did we win?"

"We didn't win overall," said Polly quietly, "but we did win our category!" Daisy pulled a large rosette from her bag and gave it to Bertie.

Bertie gave his biggest sneeze yet.

"Sounds like you've got hay fever!" said Daisy, gently stroking Bertie's feathers.

"Hay fever?" said Felicity.

"Yes, I'm prone to it myself during the summer months when I spend a lot of time with my flowers," said Daisy, rummaging in her bag.

"I didn't think! It must have started when I brought the campanula home – and I suppose taking him outside into the garden didn't help either!" said Felicity, with the sinking feeling that she had prolonged Bertie's poorly state.

Daisy pulled something out of her bag. "Don't worry. I've got a very special handkerchief in here. It will help the hay fever go away. Bertie can borrow it if you like – after all, we wouldn't have won the competition without him!"

Bertie fluffed up his feathers with pride and after a large blow on Daisy's handkerchief, immediately started to feel better.

"Maybe next summer, we should do more indoor activities!" Felicity said, with a wink at Bertie.

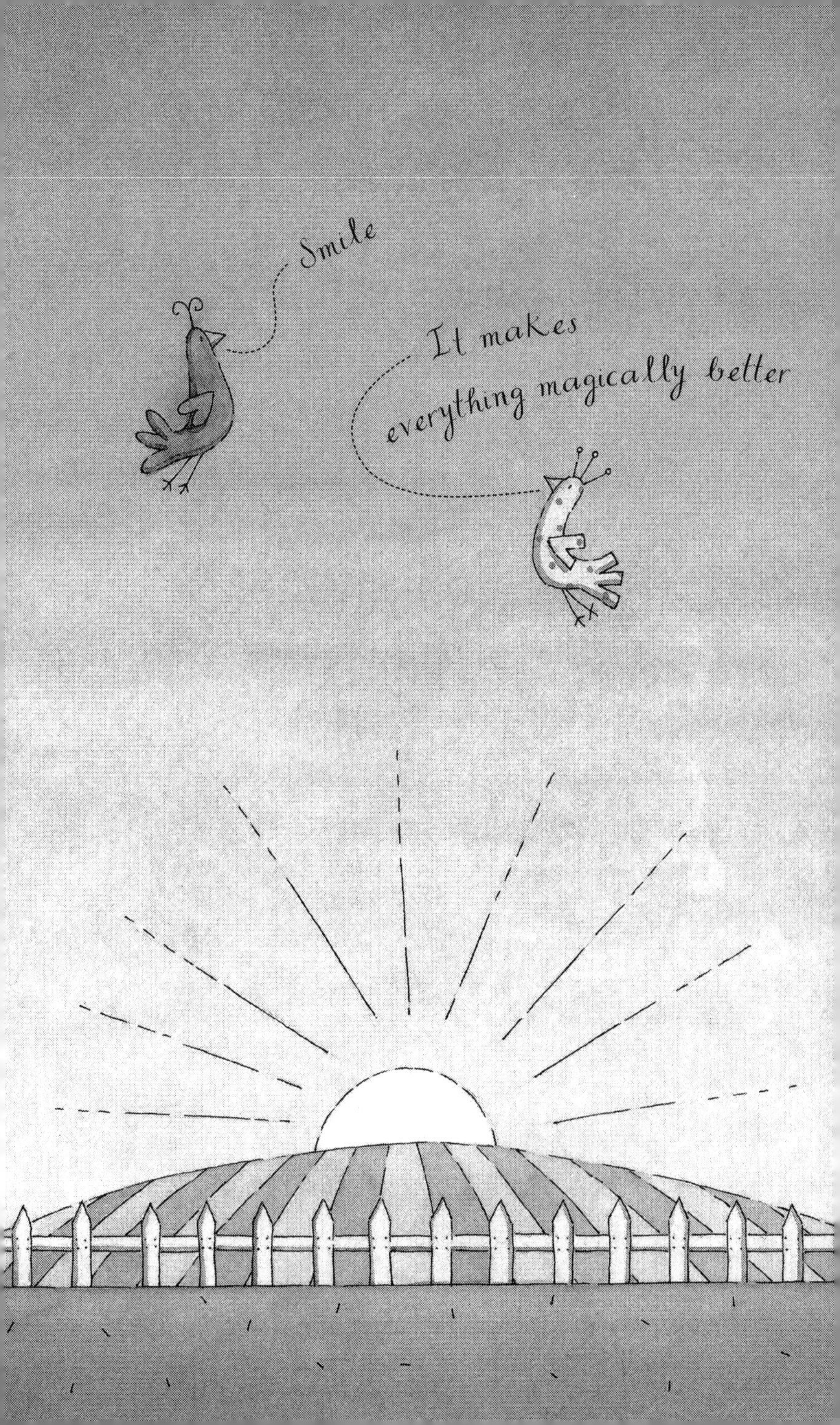
Smile
It makes everything magically better

Emma Thomson's
felicity Wishes®

It's the start of the fairies'

summer adventure, but it's

not long before their plans

start to go wrong in

Summer Sunshine

Summer Sunshine

Felicity and her best friends, Holly, Polly, Daisy and Winnie, were beside themselves with excitement. Despite being squashed uncomfortably beneath enormous heavy backpacks, their fairy wings quivered with anticipation.

"I've been looking forward to this day for so long!" squealed Felicity as she landed beside her friends in the train station with a fairylike thud.

"I never thought it would actually arrive," said Winnie excitedly. "And now it has, I can hardly believe it!"

Winnie was at school with Felicity, Holly, Polly and Daisy. She wanted to be an Adventure Fairy when she graduated. It had been her idea, one lunchtime, that they all go inter-railing around Fairy World together that summer.

At first Daisy wasn't very keen. She loved her home more than anything and never ventured far from it. The flowers in her garden needed constant care and attention.

Holly had been equally sceptical. She prided herself on being the most fashionable fairy in Little Blossoming but in the big, wide, fairy world, Holly was worried that she wouldn't stand out.

"I think it will be fun!" said Polly, encouraging her friends. "Just think of all the amazing places that we'll be able to see for real, instead of in a geography text book."

"A whole month of new experiences and adventures!" cried Winnie, bouncing up and down.

"And memories that will stay with us forever!" added Felicity dreamily.

* * *

"Has everyone got their tickets?" asked Winnie, taking charge.

"Yes!" chorused Holly, Polly, and Daisy, waggling them in the air.

"I think so!" flapped Felicity, frantically unzipping every pocket on her rucksack. "Oh, no!" she muttered hastily under her breath.

"Um… Felicity!" said Polly, trying to get her friend's attention.

"Hold on a second," said Felicity, getting more flustered by the minute as every pocket she emptied revealed no ticket.

Polly, Holly, Daisy and Winnie stared in amazement as Felicity rummaged through the most bizarre items they had ever seen packed in a suitcase! Four bags of strawberry fizzy laces, a bird bath, two mobile phones (just in case she lost one and couldn't speak to her friends), ten pairs of stripy tights and a dozen sparkle bars!

"Felicity!" said Polly sternly, trying to get her attention. "Look!"

Felicity stopped and looked up at Polly, who was waving two tickets.

"You gave me your ticket to look after... remember!"

Felicity flushed bright pink. She was notorious for forgetting things, especially when they were important.

* * *

With their tickets stamped and their bags carefully stowed away in the overhead shelves, the five fairy friends settled down for the exciting journey ahead.

"I hope no one else joins us!" said Holly, lounging luxuriously across the spare seat next to her.

Just then the compartment door swung open.

"Hello!" said a little voice. "Is this carriage number 57?"

Holly quickly jumped up. "Um, yes, yes. Is this your seat? I was just, um, keeping it warm for you," she said as she slid over to her own seat, her cheeks a little flushed.

"Hello!" said Felicity, excited to meet a new friend. "I'm Felicity and these are my best friends, Holly, Polly, Daisy and Winnie. We're going on a backpacking holiday around Fairy World. We're going to Dreamland, Bird Island and Shoe Mountain. There are so many places to visit, and so little time. Where are you going?"

To Felicity's amazement, the little fairy said nothing in return. Felicity watched as she started to unpack a book from her bag, kick off her shoes and curl up in her seat. It wasn't until the little fairy reached into her bag and pulled out Suzi Sparkle's latest CD that Felicity realised she was listening to a CD player and hadn't heard anything Felicity had said!

"Oh well, there's plenty of time to make friends during the journey," thought Felicity to herself, dying to know more about the fairy in their compartment.

* * *

As the train slowly fluttered out of Little Blossoming, the fairies left behind the billowing green hills and were soon soaring past long golden beaches, magnificent valleys and breathtaking forests.

"The view is incredible!" said Holly, mesmerized by the changing landscape.

"Just amazing," said Felicity, feeling the chug chug of the train rocking against her tired wings.

"I'm exhausted," yawned Polly, "and we haven't even been anywhere yet!"

The excitement of the trip had drained each of the fairy friends. Ever so slowly, as every mile passed, the fairies grew sleepier and sleepier, until at last the only one who was awake was the little fairy listening to music in the corner.

* * *

"Um, hello! Hello! Wake up! Is this your stop?" said the little fairy, rustling Felicity's hair with her wand. "Hello! Yooo, hoooo! If you don't wake up now I'm afraid you're going to miss your stop!" she said more loudly.

Read the rest of

Emma Thomson's
felicity Wishes®

Summer Sunshine

to find out whether the fairies'
trip of a lifetime has
gone wrong already!

If you enjoyed this book, why not try another of these fantastic story collections?

Designer Drama

Star Surprise

Clutter Clean-out

Newspaper Nerves

Enchanted Escape

Whispering Wishes

Friends Forever

Sensational Secrets

Happy Hobbies

Party Pickle

Wand Wishes

Dancing Dreams

13 Spooky Sleepover

14 Fashion Fiasco

15 Pink Paradise

16 Spectacular Skies

17 Dreamy Daisy

18 Perfect Polly

20

19

Holly's Hideaway

21

Winnie's Wonderland

Fairy Fun

Look out for these three special editions

Summer Sunshine

Christmas Calamity

Winter Wishes

Friends of Felicity

Alice 8 years old

My best friend in the whole world is Phoebe.
She is very kind and caring. When I feel
sick or dizzy she gets the teacher and
looks after me! We always try
to pick each other in a lesson
at school. I think a good friend
Shows every one how to
Co-operate together

Celebrate the joys of friendship with Felicity Wishes!

Felicity Wishes is an extra-special 'friendship' fairy - she's spirited, modern, always there for her friends; she's guaranteed to raise your spirits!

Do you have a friend who you'd like to nominate as your 'best friend'?

Do they make you laugh? Are they generous and kind? Why are they your best friend?

Just nominate your best friend and you could see your letter in one of Felicity Wishes' books. Plus the chance to win an exclusive Felicity Wishes prize!

Send in your letter on A4 paper, including your name and age and with a stamped self-addressed envelope to…

Felicity Wishes Friendship Competition,
Hodder Children's Books, 338 Euston Road, London, NW1 3BH

Australian readers should write to…

Hachette Children's Books
Level 17/207 Kent Street, Sydney, NSW 2000

New Zealand readers should write to…

Hachette Children's Books
PO Box 100-749 North Shore Mail Centre
Auckland, New Zealand

Closing date is 30th April 2007

Exclusive Felicity Wishes Prizes!

From January 2006, there will be a Felicity Wishes fiction book publishing each month (in Australia and New Zealand publishing from April 2006). Each title will display a different sticker on the front cover. Collect all 12 throughout the year, stick them on the reverse of the collectors' card which you'll find in *Dancing Dreams* or on the website, download from **www.felicitywishes.net.**

When you have collected all 12 stickers, just send them in to us! In return you'll be entered into a monthly, grand prize draw to receive a very exclusive Felicity Wishes prize*.

Please send in the completed card to the relevant address below and mark it for the attention of...

Felicity Wishes Collectors Competition,
Hodder Children's Books, 338 Euston Road,
London, NW1 3BH

Australian readers should write to...

Hachette Children's Books
Level 17/207 Kent Street, Sydney, NSW 2000

New Zealand readers should write to...

Hachette Children's Books
PO Box 100-749 North Shore Mail Centre
Auckland, New Zealand

* A draw to pick 50 winners each month will take place from January 2007
- last draw will take place on 30th June 2007.
Prizes will be a Felicity Wishes product which we hope you'll enjoy.
For full terms and conditions visit www.felicitywishes.net/terms

Would you like to be 'A Friend of Felicity'?

Felicity Wishes has her very own website, filled with lots of sparkly fairy fun and information about Felicity Wishes and all her fairy friends.

Just visit:

www.felicitywishes.net

to find out all about Felicity's books, sign up to newsletters, competitions, quizzes and special offers.

And if you want to show how much you adore and admire your friends, you can even send them a swish Felicity e-card for free. It will truly brighten up their day!

For full terms and conditions visit www.felicitywishes.net/terms